You Can Read, Pout-Pout Fish!

Deborah Diesen

Pictures by Greg Paprocki, based on illustrations
created by Dan Hanna for the *New York Times*–
bestselling Pout-Pout Fish books

Farrar Straus Giroux
New York

Farrar Straus Giroux Books for Young Readers
An imprint of Macmillan Publishing Group, LLC
120 Broadway, New York, NY 10271

Text copyright © 2020 by Deborah Diesen
Pictures copyright © 2020 by Farrar Straus Giroux Books for Young Readers
All rights reserved
Color separations by Embassy Graphics
Printed in China by RR Donnelley Asia Printing Solutions Ltd.,
Dongguan City, Guandong Province
Designed by Aram Kim
First edition, 2020

1 3 5 7 9 10 8 6 4 2

mackids.com

Library of Congress Control Number: 2019940840

Hardcover ISBN: 978-0-374-31288-6
Paperback ISBN: 978-0-374-31290-9

Our books may be purchased in bulk for promotional, educational, or business use.
Please contact your local bookseller or the Macmillan Corporate and Premium Sales Department
at (800) 221-7945 ext. 5442 or by email at MacmillanSpecialMarkets@macmillan.com.

Mr. Fish was about to pout.
He did not know how to read!

He felt sad.

Then he met his teacher.

"I will help you," said his teacher.

Mr. Fish met letters.
He liked them all.
He liked four of them best!

Mr. Fish met words.
He liked them all.
He liked one of them best!

BOOK

Mr. Fish met books.

He looked at pictures.

He looked at letters.

He looked at words.

He began to read!

He was happy.

But then he got stuck.

He met a very big word.
He tried.
But he could not read it.

Bluuuuuuuuuuuuuuuub!
He wanted to give up.

But he did not.
He asked for help!

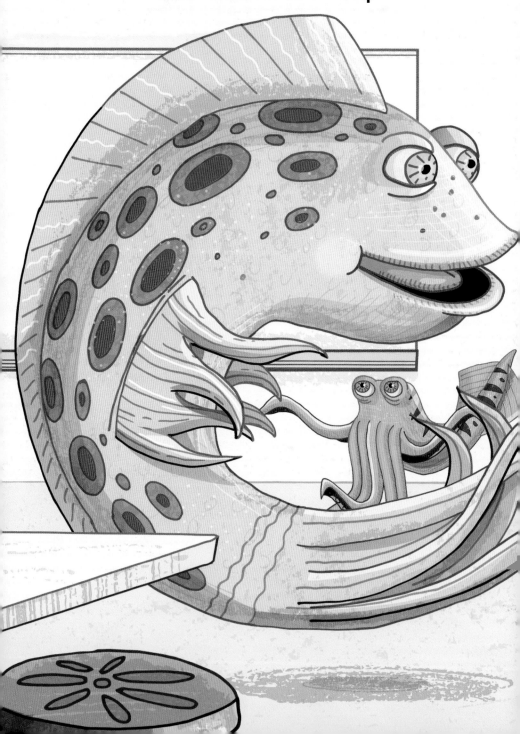

Mr. Fish and his teacher looked
at the word.
They looked at the letters.
They made sounds.

They learned the word.
Together.

Then Mr. Fish turned the page.
He kept on reading.

"I can read!" said Mr. Fish.